W9-CQP-486

AMAZING MAZES

Mind Bending Mazes
for Ages 6-60

SCHOLASTIC INC.

New York Toronto London Auckland Sydney
Mexico City New Delhi Hong Kong Buenos Aires

Rolf Heimann

No part of this publication may be reproduced in whole or in part,
or stored in a retrieval system, or transmitted in any form or by any means,
electronic, mechanical, photocopying, recording, or otherwise, without written permission of the publisher.
For information regarding permission, write to
Scholastic Inc., Attention: Permissions Department, 557 Broadway, New York, NY 10012.

ISBN 0-439-63586-1

Copyright © 1989 by Rolf Heimann.
All rights reserved.
Published by Scholastic Inc.
SCHOLASTIC and associated logos and designs are trademarks and/or
registered trademarks of Scholastic Inc.

12 11 10 9 8 7 6 5 4 3 2 1   4 5 6 7 8 9/0

Printed in China   40

First Scholastic printing, February 2004

First published in USA by Watermill Press
Produced by Reader's Digest Children's Books

Amazing History

The world's most famous maze is without a doubt the "labyrinth" of ancient Minoan mythology. It was built by Daedalus to imprison the "Minotaur," a man-eating monster. Whoever entered the labryrinth could abandon all hope of ever finding the way out. People were forced into its dark passages to be devoured by the Minotaur as human sacrifices.

The Athenian prince, Theseus, finally volunteered to be sacrificed, secretly planning to slay the monster. He succeeded in doing so and even found his way out with the aid of a long thread given to him by Ariadne, the king's daughter who had fallen in love with Theseus.

The story is, of course, a legend. But archaeologists were surprised when they excavated the ruins of Minoan palaces in the island of Crete. The intricate layouts of these palaces – some with as many as 1500 rooms – reminded them of mazes.

Many civilizations throughout the ages used mazes, usually for amusement. Even today we have fairgrounds that feature mirror mazes and people pay good money for the fun of getting lost! Modern scientists use mazes as part of intelligence tests for animals, as well as for people.

Hundreds of years ago, architects often incorporated maze designs in the decoration of churches and other buildings. They looked upon these designs, with their confusing paths and many dead-ends, as symbols of our journey through life. Often we are in doubt about which path to take! Sometimes it is only a lucky guess that puts us on the right track. But even if we meet one dead-end after another we must not get disheartened.

Lila, Tom and Ben are confronted by all sorts of mazes in this book. Some are very easy and some are quite difficult. Lila is the oldest and will attempt the hardest ones. Ben, the youngest, will do the easier ones while Tom goes for those in between.

My name–"CONNY"– is somehow hidden on every page of this book. There it is, in the corner!

1 The Labyrinth

Lila, Tom and Ben are visiting a film studio—and what a thrill it is! Tom recognizes the famous film star Miss Lemour and asks for her autograph.

"Sure honey," she says, "but be a darling and plug in my hair dryer. It must be one of those cables over there..."

Miss Lemour hasn't even noticed that her poodle, Fifi, has wandered off onto the film set. Ben discovers Fifi but can't reach her, even when he stands on the sign. Will the dog be able to get back to where the ladder leans against the wall?

In the meantime Lila hears distressed calls from two workmen who have been putting finishing touches to the Minotaur's Maze. Now they can't find their way out!

From the top of the ladder Lila should be able to guide them back.

Solution on page 29

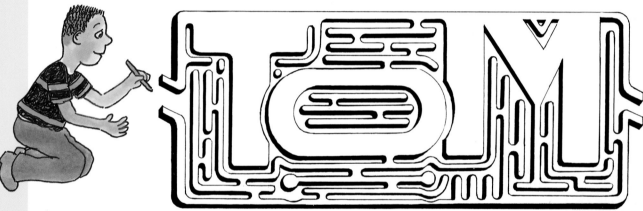

2 Drinks in the Pipeline

Lila, Tom and Ben are thirsty. There are three glasses near the lower tanks. But what sort of juice do these tanks hold? The children will have to work it out by following the pipes. Ben likes orange juice, Tom wants apple and Lila feels like some lemonade.

Solution on page 29

Here's a hint, Lila: when you come to a junction, go with the even numbers...

3 Professor McQueen's Breakfast Machine

Professor McQueen is an inventor who wants to make housework easier. At the moment he is tinkering with a machine that pours the tea and adds milk and sugar. He is very proud of his invention.

But maybe he got a bit carried away this time. He can't even remember which lever operated what and whether he was to push or to pull. In desperation he asks Lila to check his patented sugar dispenser, Tom to work out how the milk is added and Ben to check the tea-pouring mechanism.

Solution on page 29

8

4 Matching Socks

Now that they have finished washing their clothes, Ben, Tom and Lila have to find their way to the clothesline so that they can match up their socks. Start on the white platform where the odd socks are lying.

Solution on page 29

Ben can get the blue socks, Tom the green and I the yellow ones...

That looks easy. Finding my name is a lot harder!

Make your way to the bird bath using only the stepping stones that spell out the names of birds.

Solution on page 28

Stop! What's the password? You'll find it by spelling out the eight words below

Solution on page 28

5 Puzzling Picnic

Ben, Tom and Lila have climbed the lookout tower to check the park's layout before setting out to buy a few more things for their picnic on the lawn.

Ben decides to take the red boat to the lemonade stand while Tom will take the other boat to buy some apples. In the meantime, Lila will go by foot to the ice cream parlor.

Solution on page 30

Want some help in making sense of the signposts? The tip is "code word ice cream"

Step only on the panels that contain objects that begin with A. For example: apple, arrow . . .

And if you get stuck, *some* of these words might help: atom, aardvark, ape, avocado, Australia, armor, asp, ankle, antlers, awning and antique.

Solution on page 28

6 The Coolangatoo

The good old *Coolangatoo* is not the most efficient ship. In fact Captain Crabweed needs all the help he can get to run it. When his cap falls onto the foredeck he asks Ben to bring it up to him. Ben has quite a job finding his way up to the bridge.

Then the Captain wants to give three short blasts on the whistle, but the rope has broken! He sends Tom into the engine room to operate the whistle from there. Can you help Tom find the right pipe?

Lila has the hard job. She will have to untangle the telephone lines that connect the bridge to the ship below. They are in a real mess! Start with the engine room line.

Solution on page 30

Solution on page 28

15

16

7 Go Fly a Kite

Flying kites is a lot of fun, but not when they get stuck in a tree like this!

"Stay where you are!" cries the owner of the garden. "I don't want you to damage my precious Himalayan Spine Tree. Just tell me which kite is yours and I'll get it for you."

Can you work out the owner of each kite?

Solution on page 30

A quiet Sunday stroll to the park . . .

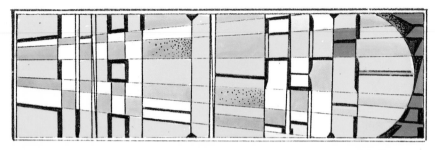

My art teacher wants me to look at the painting "Sunset in Paris". But which one is it?

If you can't work it out, check from this angle

8 Challenging Chambers

At first glance this job really looks hard. The children have to take the pegs from the center tower and fit them through the holes in the chambers until they reach the bottom.

But Lila soon finds that it's not as difficult as it looks. The objects in the chambers are a good guide.

Lila takes the round peg through the chambers that have an object starting with C - "C" for "circular."

Tom discovers that the star-shaped peg goes through the chambers that have objects starting with S.

"I can't spell!" cries Ben. But that doesn't matter. He can still recognize the diamond-shaped holes through which to push his peg.

Solution on page 30

They start with "C" too! Look out for them in "Challenging Chambers"!

9 Lasseter's Reef

Lasseter's gold reef has been rediscovered!

But it's not so easy to get there through the maze of mine shafts and tunnels. Lila, Tom and Ben have each staked a claim.

Solution on page 31

Don't forget, my name -Conny- appears on every page!

Dazzling Duet

Here are two mazes. See if you can find your way through both in under 90 seconds.

10 Log Jam

Ben will take the blue canoe and find a path through the floating logs to Middle Island, where Uncle Alf is chopping down the last three trees.

Tom will take the red canoe and bring some dry socks to Uncle Joe.

There is no canoe left for Lila. She will have to walk over the logs to Rocky Island to tell the men they have a call.

Solution on page 31

Make your way down by stepping only on the objects that are made of wood.

Solution on page 28

11 Tracks in the Snow

It is winter and the snow is full of tracks.

"Look!" cries Ben. "A rabbit went past here. Let's follow the paw prints and find out where it went!"

"Never mind the rabbit," says Tom. "Somebody took the nose from our snowman. And the rascal's footprints are still in the snow—let's follow them and find out who he is!"

"I don't want to waste my time on that," says Lila. "I'm following these ski tracks here. They're from my friend Elisa and I want to find out where she went."

Solution on page 31

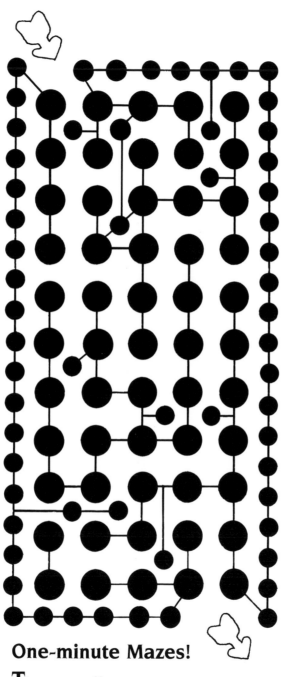

One-minute Mazes!

Time yourself
– under one minute per maze: marvelous
– under two minutes: moderate
– over two minutes: miserable!

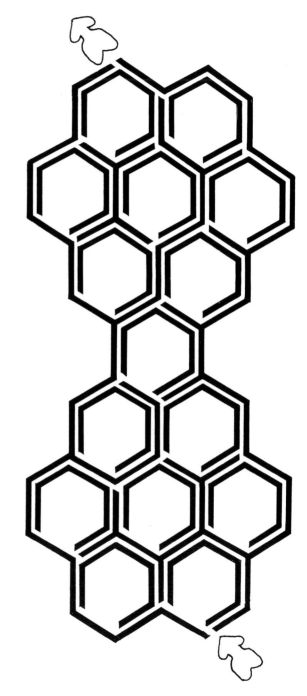

25

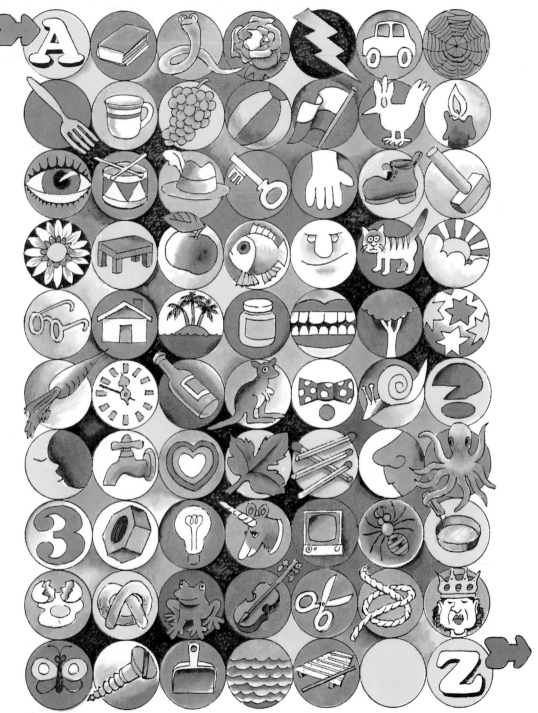

Lila wants to pick some cherries, Tom will get the plums and Ben the lemons. They should have a lot of fun finding their way to the fruit trees.

Ben will be guided by the sign of the lemons. Tom, if he keeps his eyes open, will find the whole alphabet on the way. Lila has the longest path, but if she's smart enough she will discover an encouraging message as she goes.

Solution on page 31

Step from A to Z through the entire alphabet. For example, start on A, then move to the Book for B, then to the Cup for C, and so on.

Solution on page 28

Did you know that even blind people can find their way through a maze if they stick to a simple rule? If your left hand always stays in touch with the left wall (or your right hand with the right wall) you can be sure to end up at the exit. It may take a long time but at least you can't get lost forever. Try it!

Solutions

On the next three pages you will find the solutions to the twelve main mazes. Below are the solutions to the more difficult puzzles and mazes from the other pages.

Page 11: Cockatoo, owl, lark, kookaburra, albatross, sandpiper, robin. The code word on the lower picture is SUNLIGHT.

Page 13: Apple, arrow, armor, avocado, Africa, ant, asparagus, atom, armchair, alarm clock, animal, anchor, archway, ape, airplane, arm, arrow, antlers, awning, astronaut, acorn, apple, arrow, Australia, atom, apple.

Page 14

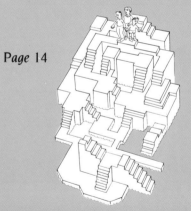

Page 23: Cradle, tree stump, chair, chest, log, table, tree, bowl, fence, gate.

Page 26: A, book, cup, drum, eye, flower, glasses, house, island, jar, kangaroo, leaf, matches, nose, octopus, pan, queen, rope, scissors, television, unicorn, violin, water, xylophone, yellow, z.

1 The Labyrinth

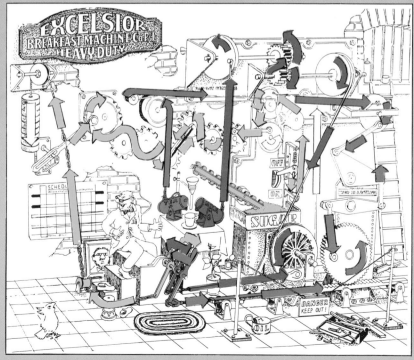

2 Drinks in the Pipeline

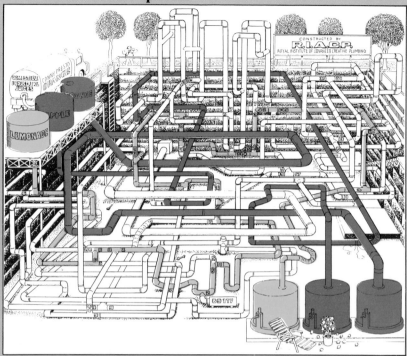

3 Professor McQueen's Breakfast Machine

4 Matching Socks

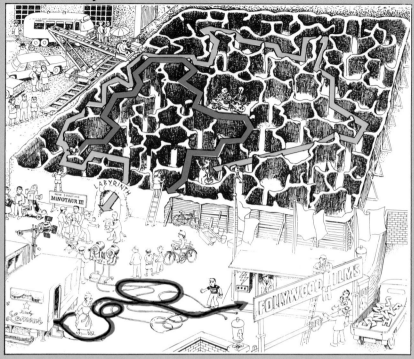

5 Puzzling Picnic

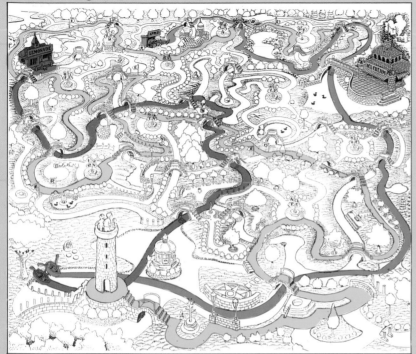

6 The Coolangatoo

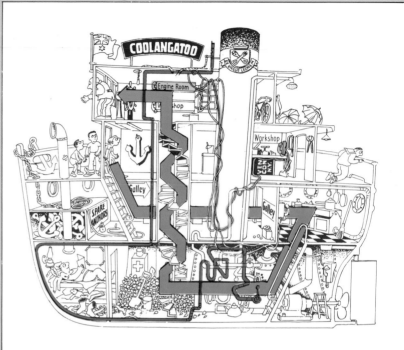

7 Go Fly a Kite

8 Challenging Chambers

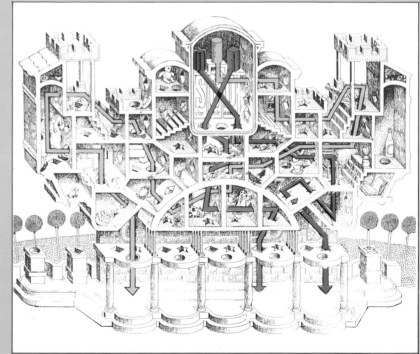